Published in the United States by Grolier Books,
a division of Grolier Enterprises, Inc.

ISBN: 0-7172-8456-5

Hiawatha
and the Big Flood

GROLIER
BOOKS

Hiawatha was a small Indian brave.
He loved the forest very much.
All the forest animals were his friends.

His best friends were the beavers.

Hiawatha liked to watch them work on their dam.

Sometimes the beavers gathered sticks for the dam.

Sometimes they cut down trees
with their strong teeth.

Hiawatha loved to play with his friends.
But he also wished to be grown up.
Then he could hunt with the braves!

One night the Indians were sitting
around the campfire.

The braves were planning a bear hunt
for the next day.

"I want to go too,"
said Hiawatha.

The braves smiled.

Early the next morning the braves
were ready to leave.

"I'm ready too," Hiawatha said.

"YOU go on a bear hunt?" said a brave.
"You are still too small, Hiawatha. Stay
near the camp and play."

Off marched the braves
on their hunt.

Hiawatha sadly watched
them go.

"Come gather berries with me," said his sister, Sunflower.

"That is for children," said Hiawatha. "I want to be a brave."

And he walked off by himself.

Hiawatha climbed a tall tree.
From the top he could see the braves.
They were marching down the path to
the big river.

The braves marched past
the beavers' dam.

Then they crossed the big river
on a log bridge.
The bridge was made from a fallen tree.

The braves reached the other side of the river.

They disappeared behind a cliff.

"I wish I could go with them," Hiawatha said to himself.

Suddenly rain began to fall.

Hiawatha climbed down the tree.

He headed back to the camp.

Hiawatha ran home quickly in the rain.
His forest friends ran for shelter.
The lightning was bright.
The thunder was loud.

Hiawatha was soaking wet when he
reached his tepee.

Sunflower and his mother were waiting
for him.

"Take off those wet things," said
Hiawatha's mother.
She hung up his clothes to dry.

"Braves don't care if they get wet,"
said Hiawatha.

Hiawatha ate a bowl of good hot stew.
"I wonder where the braves are now,"
he said.

"I wish they were home," said his mother.
"This is bad weather for hunting."

All night long the rain poured down
on the Indian camp.

The trees bent in the wind.

The river turned into a roaring flood.

The flood swept away the beavers' dam.
It swept the beaver family right
out of their beds!

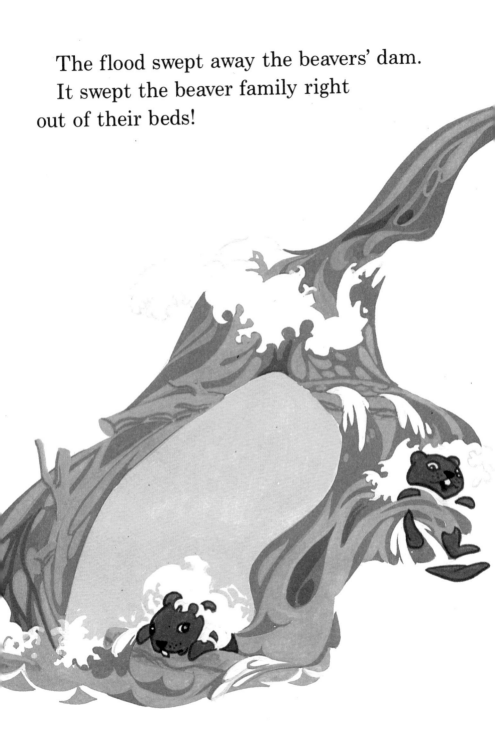

In the morning the rain
stopped.
    The beavers saw
an amazing sight!

The braves were trapped on a big rock
in the middle of the river.
The flood had swept away the log bridge.

Now the Indian braves could not cross
the river.
They could not get home!

Back at the camp the Indians were waking up.

"The rain has stopped. The braves will soon be home," said Hiawatha's mother.

But the braves did not come.
Hours went by.
The women were very worried.

"Something has happened to the braves,"
Hiawatha told his friends the rabbits.
"They have not come home from the hunt."

Hiawatha ran to the river.
The rabbits hopped along with him.

When Hiawatha reached the river, he saw
that the braves were trapped.
"I must help them!"
said Hiawatha. "But how?"

Then the braves saw Hiawatha.
"Help, help!" they called to him.
"What can I do?" Hiawatha called back.

"Catch this rope!" called a brave.
He flung it toward Hiawatha.
But the rope was too short.

"We need a new bridge!" called another brave. "Can you cut down that tree?"

Hiawatha looked at the big tree.
How could he chop down a tree all by himself?
"I must do my best!" he thought.

Chip! Chip!
went Hiawatha's ax
into the tree bark.

"This is hard work,"
said Hiawatha.
The beavers came
over to watch him.

"This ax will never
do the job," Hiawatha
said to the beavers.

The beavers were happy to help.
Chomp, chomp!
They chewed away at the tree with
their strong teeth.

Soon the tall tree
began to sway.
    "Careful!" said
Hiawatha.

Hiawatha pushed the tree so it would fall
across the river.
    The beavers pushed too.

CRASH!

The tall tree reached all the way
to the rock.

It became a long, strong bridge
for the braves.

The happy braves cheered loudly.
"Hooray for Hiawatha!" they cried.

The braves came back across the river
on the new bridge.

Hiawatha was the hero of the day!

Hiawatha rode back to the Indian camp
on the shoulders of a brave.

The big chief gave Hiawatha a war bonnet.
"You saved the lives of the braves,"
the big chief said to Hiawatha. "I am
very proud of you."
"The beavers helped too," said Hiawatha.

The next day Hiawatha and
Sunflower went back to the river.
They helped the beaver family
to rebuild their dam.

By sunset the work was finished.

Hiawatha and Sunflower waved good-bye to their friends.

And the beavers waved back.

Everyone was safe and happy!